Smithsonian Prehistoric Zone

Ankylosaurus

by Gerry Bailey
Illustrated by Adrian Chesterman

Crabtree Publishing Company

www.crabtreebooks.com

Crabtree Publishing Company

www.crabtreebooks.com

Author
Gerry Bailey

Proofreaders
Crystal Sikkens
Kathy Middleton

Illustrator
Adrian Chesterman

Prepress technician
Samara Parent

Editorial coordinator
Kathy Middleton

Editor
Lynn Peppas

Print and production coordinator
Katherine Berti

Ankylosaurus, originally published as *Ankylosaurus Fights Back* by Laura Gates Galvin, Illustrated by Adrian Chesterman
Book copyright © 2007 Trudy Corporation and the Smithsonian Institution, Washington DC 20560.

Library of Congress Cataloging-in-Publication Data

Bailey, Gerry.
   Ankylosaurus / by Gerry Bailey ; illustrated by Adrian Chesterman.
      p. cm. -- (Smithsonian prehistoric zone)
   Includes index.
   ISBN 978-0-7787-1810-9 (pbk. : alk. paper) -- ISBN 978-0-7787-1797-3 (reinforced library binding : alk. paper) -- ISBN 978-1-4271-9701-6 (electronic (pdf))
   1. Ankylosaurus--Juvenile literature. I. Title. II. Series.

   QE862.O65B343 2011
   567.915--dc22

                     2010044024

Library and Archives Canada Cataloguing in Publication

Bailey, Gerry
   Ankylosaurus / by Gerry Bailey ; illustrated
by Adrian Chesterman.

(Smithsonian prehistoric zone)
Includes index.
At head of title: Smithsonian Institution.
Issued also in electronic format.
ISBN 978-0-7787-1797-3 (bound).-- ISBN 978-0-7787-1810-9 (pbk.)

      1. Ankylosaurus--Juvenile literature.
I. Chesterman, Adrian II. Smithsonian Institution
III. Title. IV. Series: Bailey, Gerry. Smithsonian prehistoric zone.

QE862.O65B33 2011   j567.915   C2010-906880-7

Crabtree Publishing Company

www.crabtreebooks.com   1-800-387-7650
Copyright © **2011 CRABTREE PUBLISHING COMPANY**.
All rights reserved. No part of this publication may be reproduced, stored in a retrieval system or be transmitted in any form or by any means, electronic, mechanical, photocopying, recording, or otherwise, without the prior written permission of Crabtree Publishing Company. In Canada: we acknowledge the financial support of the Government of Canada through the Canada Book Fund for our publishing activities.

Published in the United States
Crabtree Publishing
PMB 59051
350 Fifth Avenue, 59th Floor
New York, New York 10118

Published in Canada
Crabtree Publishing
616 Welland Ave.
St. Catharines, Ontario
L2M 5V6

Printed in China/012011/GW20101014

Dinosaurs

Living things had been around for billions of years before dinosaurs came along. Animal life on Earth started with single-cell **organisms** that lived in the seas. About 380 million years ago, some animals came out of the sea and onto the land. These were the ancestors that would become the mighty dinosaurs.

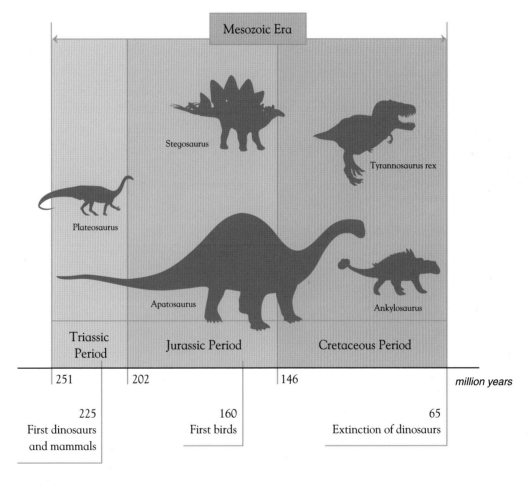

Mesozoic Era

Stegosaurus

Tyrannosaurus rex

Plateosaurus

Apatosaurus

Ankylosaurus

Triassic Period	Jurassic Period	Cretaceous Period

251	202	146	*million years*

225 First dinosaurs and mammals	160 First birds	65 Extinction of dinosaurs

The dinosaur era is called the Mesozoic era. It is divided into three parts called the Triassic, Jurassic, and Cretaceous periods. Flowering plants grew for the first time during the Cretaceous period. Plant-eating dinosaurs, such as *Ankylosaurus* and *Triceratops*, flourished. *Albertosaurus* and *Tyrannosaurus rex*, fed on the plant-eaters. Dinosaurs (except birds)were wiped out by the end of the Cretaceous period. No one is sure exactly why.

Ankylosaurus roamed Earth millions of years ago.
It was warm and humid. The land was covered in
scrubby plants, small trees, flowers, and ferns.

Ankylosaurus wandered
close to the river where
there was a lot of plants.

Ankylosaurus was a large, wide-bodied dinosaur that walked on all four of its short, strong legs. It was a **herbivore**, or plant-eater, and spent most of the day grazing on plants. Its mouth was wide and flat with a beak that could tear plants. It had to eat a lot of plants to get all the **nutrition** it needed.

For protection, Ankylosaurus was covered in large bony plates that acted like a suit of armor. At the end of its tail were two **knob**-shaped bones.

It also had spikes along
its body that stuck out
as a warning to attackers.

Other plant-eating dinosaurs lived
alongside Ankylosaurus such as the swift,
delicate Ornithomimus. Other animals
besides dinosaurs lived here as well.

Pteranodon, a huge pterosaur, flew
in the air on huge wings. There were
even hungry crocodiles swimming in
warm rivers at that time.

The meat-eating dinosaurs were fierce
attackers. Their **prey** included other
smaller meat-eaters, as well as the gentler
plant-eaters such as Ankylosaurus.

Some of these **predators** were hunters. The mighty
Tyrannosaurus rex was one of these predators.
Other dinosaurs were **scavengers** that lived off
animals that other dinosaurs had killed.

Ankylosaurus was well prepared to fight off predators such as Tyrannosaurus rex because it had a special weapon. At the end of its tail grew large knobs of **fused** bone that it used as a club. It could swing the club from side to side and do terrible damage to anything it hit. Its back legs and hips had to be very strong to support such a heavy tail.

Animals such as Tyrannosaurus rex towered over Ankylosaurus. It used its razor-sharp teeth and strong jaws to try to bite through the Ankylosaurus's armor. But it was no use.

The armor was too strong. All the
meat-eater could do was try to turn
Ankylosaurus over on its back to
get at its soft underside.

But Ankylosaurus was ready for this too. When attacked, he could flatten itself against the ground to protect its underside. It could also turn away from the predator and swing its club tail. As the tail swung heavily from side to side, it became a powerful weapon.

If the club end of the tail hit its target it could cause a lot of damage to the attacker. It could even break bones. Even a fierce **carnivore** such as Tyrannosaurus rex would be **wary** of attacking an Ankylosaurus unless it was very hungry. A broken leg would stop Tyrannosaurus rex from hunting and weaken it in fighting off other meat-eaters.

Once Ankylosaurus had injured its attacker it could escape. Ankylosaurus was not very fast but it was quick enough to get away from an injured predator.

Now it would have to look for another safe
place to eat. It took an awful lot of plant food
to satisfy Ankylosaurus and its big appetite.

Many of the tough plants Ankylosaurus ate were hard to **digest**. It is possible that Ankylosaurus digested its meals slowly. This gave the plants time to **ferment** inside its body.

This helped Ankylosaurus digest rough material, but it also made the dinosaur produce a lot of gas. This probably made it one of the smelliest animals too!

All about Ankylosaurus

(ang-KIE-lo-SORE-us)

The *Ankylosaurus* lived more than 65 million years ago near the end of the Cretaceous period which stretched from 144 million years ago to around 65 million years ago. The Cretaceous was part of the Mesozoic era. By the end of the Cretaceous period, dinosaurs had been wiped out.

The name *Ankylosaurus* means "fused lizard" and refers to its armor-plated skin. It was 25 to 35 feet (7.6 to 10.7 meters) long, 5.5 feet (1.7 meters) wide, and approximately four feet (1.3 meters) high. It weighed about five tons (4.5 metric tons)! The largest *Ankylosaurus* skull found so far is over two feet (64.5 cm) long and almost 2.5 feet (74.5 cm) wide.

The body of an *Ankylosaurus* was covered with bony plates set close together in thick, leathery skin. These plates helped protect the plant-eater from predators. *Ankylosaurus* had a bony club at the end of its tail that it could swing back and forth to defend itself.

Precambrian Era		570 million years ago			Palaeozoic Era		
Precambrian Period		Cambrian Period	Ordovician Period	Silurian Period	Devonian Period		Carboniferous

380
First life on land

320
First reptiles

The club was connected to seven joined **vertebrae**. It was stiff and strong. Bony **tendons** added extra support when the *Ankylosaurus* swung its tail.

Bony knobs and spikes protected its head. The bones in its head were covered with extra armor. It even had bony plates over its eyelids.

Ankylosaurus was not very intelligent when compared to other dinosaurs. It had a useful suit of armor and spent most of its time grazing for food. It did not need to be too smart.

The *Ankylosaurus* was a herbivore, which means it ate only plants. It cropped large amounts of food using its beak-like mouth. Scientists think it used fermentation to help it digest the tough plant material it lived on. This way of digestion could have caused *Ankylosaurus* to produce an enormous amount of gas.

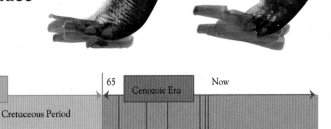

		248				65		Now
				Mesozoic Era			Cenozoic Era	
Period	Permian Period	Triassic Period	Jurassic Period		Cretaceous Period			

1.8
First humans

Ankylosaurus and family

Ankylosaurus was just one member of the *Ankylosauria*, which included most of the big armored dinosaurs. It is split into two families. One is called *Ankylosauridae*, and the other is called *Nodosauridae*. *Ankylosaurids* had a club on the end of their tail. Nodosaurids did not have a club.

The *armadillo* and the *pangolin* are two armored mammals that exist today. *Armadillos* appeared around 60 million years ago. *Pangolins* appeared around 40 million years ago.

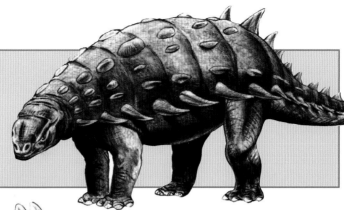

Name: *Hylaeosaurus*
Family: Nodosauridae
Time: Early Cretaceous
Size: 20 feet (6 meters)
Location: Europe

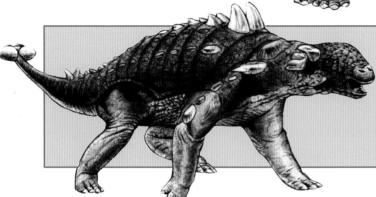

Name: *Euoplocephalus*
Family: Ankylosauridae
Time: Late Cretaceous
Size: 13 feet (4 meters)
Location: Canada

Armored animals of today

Name: armadillo (*Dasypus*)
Family: Dasypodidae
Size: 4–5 feet (1–1.5 m)
Location: Southern USA, South and Central America

Name: pangolin (*Manis*)
Family: Manidae
Size: 2–2.5 feet (54–80 cm)
Location: East and Southeast Asia, East and Southern Africa

Dinosaur brains

Most dinosaurs were about as intelligent as a crocodile. Some were smarter than others. Scientists calculate how intelligent a dinosaur might have been by measuring its brain size compared to its body weight. This is called its *EQ*. It stands for *Encephalization Quotient*.

The *Ankylosaurus* was not very far up the chart. It measured 0.5, which means its brain size was small compared to its weight. It probably was not as intelligent as the *troodontids* or *dromaeosaurids* at the top of the chart. They measured up to 5.8. *Sauropods*, such as the huge *Diplodocus*, measured a low 0.1 to 0.2 on the EQ chart. This probably had more to do with the *sauropod's* enormous size than it's lack of intelligence.

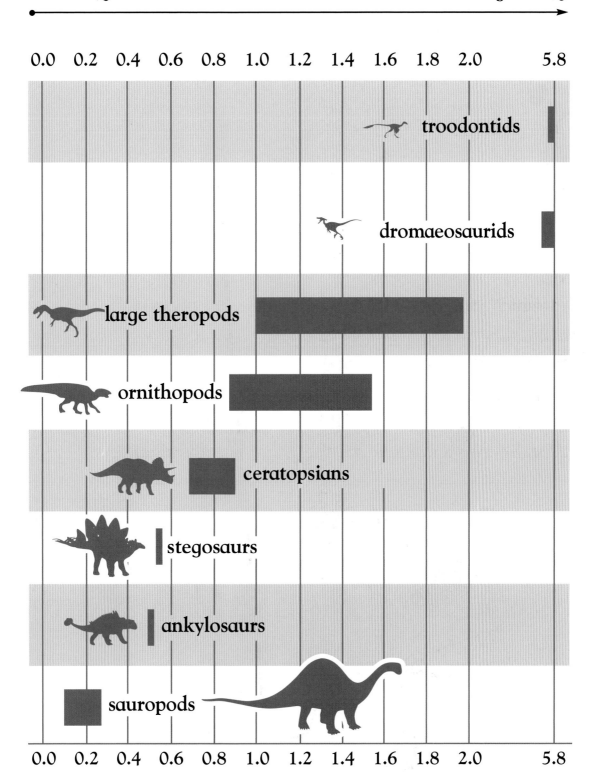

lowest EQ   highest EQ

0.0 0.2 0.4 0.6 0.8 1.0 1.2 1.4 1.6 1.8 2.0   5.8

troodontids

dromaeosaurids

large theropods

ornithopods

ceratopsians

stegosaurs

ankylosaurs

sauropods

0.0 0.2 0.4 0.6 0.8 1.0 1.2 1.4 1.6 1.8 2.0   5.8

Glossary

carnivore A meat-eater, to feed on another animals' flesh

digest To break down and change food so that it can be absorbed by the body

ferment To go through a state of change

fuse Joined together or united as if one

herbivore A plant-eating animal

knob A rounded area that sticks out

nutrition The process of taking in food to be used by living things

organisms Any living animal or plant

predator An animal that hunts other animals for food

prey Animals that are hunted by other animals for food

pterosaur Flying reptiles that lived from the late Triassic period (220 million years ago) to the Cretaceous period

scavengers An animal that feeds on the remains of dead animals

tendon The tissue that connects muscle to bone

vertebrae The bones that make up the backbone of an animal

wary Careful or cautious

Index

Further Reading and Websites

Ankylosaurus: The Armored Dinosaur by David West and Nick Spender. (2009)

Ankylosaurus and Other Armored and Plated Herbivores (Dinosaurs!) by David West. (2010)

Ankylosaurus Fights Back (Smithsonian's Prehistoric Pals) by Laura Gates Galvin (2007)

Websites:

www.enchantedlearning.com/subjects/dinosaurs/

http://kids.nationalgeographic.com/kids/animals/creaturefeature/ankylosaurus-magniventris/

www.smithsonianeducation.org